Waiting-for-Christmas Stories

Waiting-for-Christmas Stories

By Bethany Roberts
Illustrated by Sarah Stapler

Clarion Books/*New York*

Clarion Books
a Houghton Mifflin Company imprint
215 Park Avenue South, New York, NY 10003
Text copyright © 1994 by Barbara Beverage
Illustrations copyright © 1994 by Sarah Stapler

The illustrations for this book were executed in watercolor
on Bristol board
The text was set in 14/19 pt. Cochin

Printed in the USA

Library of Congress Cataloging-in-Publication Data

Roberts, Bethany.
    Waiting-for-Christmas stories / by Bethany Roberts ; illustrated
by Sarah Stapler.
        p. cm.
    Summary: Papa Rabbit tells his children seven bedtime stories
on Christmas Eve.
    ISBN 0-395-67324-0
    [1. Christmas—Fiction. 2. Storytelling—Fiction. 3. Bedtime—
Fiction. 4. Rabbits—Fiction.] I. Stapler, Sarah, ill. II. Title.
    PZ7.R5396Waf 1995
    [E]—dc20
                                                    93-11480
                                                        CIP
                                                         AC

WOZ 10 9 8 7 6 5 4 3 2 1

It is Christmas eve. As the fire crackles in the fireplace and candles glow softly in the windows, the little rabbits are tucked into bed, ready to hear Waiting-for-Christmas stories.

Papa pulls up a rocking chair, clears his throat, and storytime begins.

CHRISTMAS LETTERS

One snowy day before Christmas, a little rabbit went to the mailbox. He opened it and looked inside. But there was nothing in it.

"I wish I would get a Christmas letter," he said.

"If you would write a letter, you would get a letter," said the mailbox.

"I don't know what to write," said the little rabbit.

"How do you feel?" asked the mailbox.

"I feel bouncy and happy and Christmasy."

"Write that," said the mailbox. "What are you thinking about?"

"I am thinking about my grandma's yummy Christmas pies."

"Write that," said the mailbox. "And what did you do today?"

"I looked inside the mailbox, but there was nothing in it."

"Write that!" said the mailbox.

So the little rabbit sat down and wrote a Christmas letter to his grandma. He mailed it right away.

Then he waited to get a letter back.

Day after day he checked the mailbox.

But day after day the mailbox was still empty.

"No letter," sighed the little rabbit.

"No letter," sighed the mailbox.

And then, one day, there was a letter!

"A letter for me!" cried the little rabbit.

"Read it! Read it!" cried the mailbox.

"Dear Grandson,

Thank you for your letter.
Christmas is coming,
and I will see you soon!

Love,
Grandma Rabbit

P.S. I am baking a Christmas pie,
just for you!"

"You were right, Mailbox!" shouted the little rabbit. "I wrote a letter, and I got a letter."

"A letter for a letter, I always say!" said the mailbox.

CHRISTMAS COOKIES

Mama Rabbit decided to bake cookies for Christmas.

"Now let's see," she said. "How should I make them?"

"Mix," said the spoon.

"Roll," said the rolling pin.

"Cut," said the cutters.

"Pop them in here," said the oven.

"R-RING! Take them out! Don't let them burn!" cried the clock.

Mama Rabbit mixed and rolled and cut, and popped cookies in and out of the oven as fast as she could.

Soon the table was piled high with cookies.

"Mix more!" said the spoon.

"Roll again!" cried the rolling pin.

"Cut! Cut! Cut!" shouted the cutters.

14

"Pop them in here!" yelled the oven.

"R-RRRRING!" shrieked the clock.

So Mama Rabbit rushed about and made more cookies.

Mix! Roll! Cut! Pop! R-RRRRING!

Mix! Roll! Cut! Pop! R-RRRRING!

Mama Rabbit scurried faster and faster.

She made more and more cookies.

Mix! Roll! Cut! Pop! R-RRRRING!

Mix! Roll! Cut! Pop! R-RRRRING!

Before long, cookies were stacked on the counter, heaped on chairs, tucked into drawers, piled on the windowsill, and crammed into all the cupboards.

"*Stop!*" cried Mama Rabbit. "There is not room in this kitchen for one more cookie!"

"*Twee-eeeet!*" whistled the teapot. "Time for tea!"

"Yes," said Mama Rabbit, "I do believe it is." And she sat down and had a Christmas cookie with her tea.

THE CHRISTMAS PACKAGE

Papa Rabbit was wrapping a package. He used green paper. He used red ribbon.

Just as he was tying the ribbon into a nice, big bow, the package said, "*Ouch!* That is too tight!"

"Sorry," said Papa Rabbit. "Let me try again. Is that better?"

"I suppose so," grumbled the package. "And now I bet you are going to stuff me into a closet, full of other boxes."

"No," said Papa Rabbit. "I am going to put you under the Christmas tree."

"Sure, sure!" said the package. "Knocked around, bumped, squeezed and shoved. That's the life of a box."

"But you are not just a box anymore," said Papa Rabbit. "You are a Christmas package."

"Big deal," muttered the package.

"Well, then," said Papa Rabbit, "I guess you don't want to know."

"Know what?" asked the package.

"You don't want to know your secret," said Papa Rabbit.

"My secret?" said the package.

"Yes," said Papa Rabbit. "Inside, you have a secret."

"Tell me, tell me my secret!" cried the package.

So Papa Rabbit unwrapped the package and took off the top. He showed the package the secret inside.

"I have a secret!" shouted the package.

"A Christmas secret," said Papa Rabbit. "You'll be the best Christmas package ever."

"The *best!*" agreed the package.

A CHRISTMAS STAR

The little rabbit's sister was trimming the Christmas tree.
At the very top she put a star.

"There," she said. "Now that is perfect!"

"No, it's not," said the star. "A perfect Christmas tree
has popcorn."

"Oh," said Little Sister. So she strung some popcorn
and hung it on the tree.

"How is that?" she asked.

"Not bad," said the star, "but it needs cookie angels."

"How true," said Little Sister.

She hung some cookie angels on the tree.

"Is that better?" she asked.

"Getting better," said the star, "but it should have paper Santas."

"Right," said Little Sister.

She cut some paper Santas and put them on the tree, too.

"Is this perfect now?" she asked.

"Almost," said the star. "A perfect Christmas tree always has a present for the star."

"And what does the star want for Christmas?" asked Little Sister.

"A hat," said the star. "A hat with bells."

"Of course!" said Little Sister. "Now why didn't I think of that?"

So she made a hat with bells.

She put it on the star.

The star shook his new hat.

Jingle! Jingle! Jingle! rang the bells.

"Now *that*," said the star, "is perfect!"

THE CHRISTMAS STOCKING

On the day before Christmas, Grandpa Rabbit took a hammer and a nail to hang up his Christmas stocking. *Rat-a-tat!*

He hung his stocking next to the other stockings. But when he turned around, the stocking fell to the floor. *Whump!*

Grandpa Rabbit hung the stocking up again. And the stocking fell again. *Whump!*

Grandpa Rabbit tried a bigger nail. But the stocking fell again. Each time he hung the stocking up — *whump!* — down it fell.

"There is something wrong with this stocking!" said Grandpa Rabbit, and he walked away. But . . . *whump, whump, whump!* The stocking followed right behind him.

Grandpa Rabbit sat down on the couch. The stocking sat down next to him.

"How strange," said Grandpa Rabbit.

Grandpa Rabbit read a book. The stocking snuggled right beside him.

"This is an odd stocking," said Grandpa Rabbit.

Grandpa Rabbit played his fiddle. Two little ears popped out of the stocking to listen.

"I have never heard of a stocking with ears," said Grandpa Rabbit. "What is the matter with this stocking? I will try one more time to hang it."

Grandpa picked up the hammer and nail. *Rat-a-tat!* He hung his stocking.

"Hooray!" he cried. "This time my stocking stays up! I wonder what *was* the matter with it before?"

Just as Grandpa Rabbit sat down to think, two little ears poked out from behind a chair, and two little feet hopped away! *Whump, whump, whump!*

CHRISTMAS CAROLS

Just before Christmas, Grandma Rabbit got sick.

"Ah-choo!" she sneezed, and huddled closer to the fire.

"This is nod budge fun," said her nose, sniffling.

"Wish we could go for a walk," said her feet.

"Bor-ring," complained her ears.

Grandma Rabbit sighed and wrapped her blanket more tightly around herself.

Suddenly, the sound of singing came from outside.

"Whad's thad?" asked her nose.

"Let's go and listen," said her ears.

"Hurry, hurry!" cried her feet.

Grandma Rabbit ran to look out her window.
There, singing in the cold and the snow, were carolers.
Grandma Rabbit opened her door.
"Ah-choo!" she sneezed. "Come in!"

The carolers gathered around the fire, singing of Christmas cheer.

"Whad fun!" said Grandma Rabbit's nose.

"Goody, goody!" said her ears.

"Ah-h-h!" sighed her feet.

"What joy, joy, joy!" said Grandma Rabbit.

And with the carolers, she sang:

"Fa-la-la-la-la-la-la-ah-choo!"

CHRISTMAS GIVING

On Christmas Eve, Papa Rabbit and Mama Rabbit were almost ready for Christmas.

"I want to give Papa Rabbit a special present for Christmas," said Mama Rabbit.

"I want to give Mama Rabbit a special present for Christmas," said Papa Rabbit.

Mama Rabbit thought.

"I could give Papa a tune."

Papa Rabbit thought.

"I could give Mama a poem."

Mama Rabbit hummed and hummed.

Papa Rabbit wrote and wrote.

On Christmas day, everybody came: Grandpa, Grandma, aunts, uncles, and rabbit cousins. The family had a Christmas feast. They opened stockings and presents. They sang songs. They danced around and around the Christmas tree.

"Now let's go skating!" said Papa.

So they all put on their scarves and mittens. And they all went to the pond to skate. *Slide, glide, slide!*

As she skated, Mama Rabbit hummed her tune. Papa Rabbit read his poem. Then Mama Rabbit and Papa Rabbit put the tune and the poem together. Together, they sang this song:

> Rabbit Christmas! Rabbit joys!
> Rabbit children, girls and boys,
>   *hum-hum-hum*
> Grandpa, Grandma, me and you,
> Aunts and uncles, cousins, too!
>   *hum-hum-hum*
> Family Christmas is such fun—
> Merry Christmas, everyone!
>   *hum-hum-hum!*

As Papa Rabbit sings, the little rabbits drift off to sleep, dreaming Christmas dreams.

When they wake up, Christmas has come, at last!

"Merry Christmas!" say Papa and Mama Rabbit.

"Merry Christmas!" say Grandpa, Grandma, aunts, uncles, and cousins as they arrive at the door.

"Merry Christmas!" shout all the little rabbits.

"MERRY CHRISTMAS!"